# Fiona & Frieda's
### Fairy-tale Adventures

# Sleeping Beauty
# and the Snapdragons

by Nadia Higgins          illustrated by Meredith Johnson

magic
wagon

**visit us at www.abdopublishing.com**

Published by Magic Wagon, a division of the ABDO Group, 8000 West 78th Street, Edina, Minnesota 55439. Copyright © 2009 by Abdo Consulting Group, Inc. International copyrights reserved in all countries. All rights reserved. No part of this book may be reproduced in any form without written permission from the publisher.

Calico Chapter Books™ is a trademark and logo of Magic Wagon.

Printed in the United States.

Text by Nadia Higgins
Illustrations by Meredith Johnson
Edited by Patricia Stockland
Interior layout and design by Rebecca Daum
Cover design by Rebecca Daum

**Library of Congress Cataloging-in-Publication Data**
Higgins, Nadia.
  Sleeping Beauty and the snapdragons / by Nadia Higgins ; illustrated by Meredith Johnson.
      p. cm. — (Fiona & Frieda's fairy-tale adventures)
  ISBN 978-1-60270-576-0
  [1. Fairy tales—Fiction. 2. Characters in literature—Fiction.]
I. Johnson, Meredith, ill. II. Title.
  PZ7.H5349558Sl 2009
  [Fic]—dc22

                                        2008038554

*For my prince, Louis—N. H.*

Fiona

Frieda

# Chapter 1

**Once upon** a time in a land not far away at all (in fact, just around the corner from Sweet Nothings Bakery), there lived two third graders, Fiona and Frieda. The girls were neighbors to each other on the eighth floor of Castle Apartments. They were also both in the same class at Sprinkledust Elementary. Plus, they were best friends.

Basically, Fiona and Frieda did just about everything together. And, in their case, "everything" usually meant something to do with fairy tales. For more than pizza, more than video games, more than snow days, and even more than Saturday morning cartoons, Fiona and Frieda loved fairy tales.

But that didn't mean the girls were the same. For example, in their game Fairy-tale Adventures, they acted out famous fairy tales or ones they made up. And Fiona and Frieda always chose different roles.

As Fiona put it, she would rather "kiss a tarantula" than play some creepy witch or animal. She was always a princess, a mermaid, a kind fairy, or something lovely like that.

That suited Frieda just fine. For her part, she would rather "stare at ceiling cracks" than play one of those boring ladies. Frieda preferred the role of a snarling, drooling beast or a witch with scrunched-up lips.

One day last winter, the girls had been playing Fairy-tale Adventures when their lives changed forever.

On this day, they realized they had magic powers. All they had to do was rhyme at the same exact time. So, for example, if Fiona said "pickle" while Frieda said "tickle," something amazing happened. White magic swirled in the air, and all ordinary noises stopped. Only the voices of fairy-tale characters could now be heard. Though their world *looked* the same, it was now filled with *real* maidens and *real* witches.

Before they knew it, Fiona and Frieda realized that they were characters in the fairy tales, too. And it was up to them to save the princess or get rid of the bad guys. Their job sure wasn't easy, but luckily, the girls were fairy-tale experts. Between the two of them, they always came up with a plan—sometimes just in time. So far, they'd never had to use their magic rhyming powers to leave the fairy tales—and miss the happy ending.

Usually the girls played Fairy-tale Adventures on Saturday mornings. But this Saturday morning was special. Today the girls were busy in the kitchen. Frieda was working on a new recipe for fake smoke. And Fiona, well, she was buzzing around like a wind-up bee in an apron.

Today Fiona was making a cake—and not just any cake. It was a birthday cake—and not just any birthday cake. "For the smartest, prettiest, sweetest cousin ever," was what Fiona planned to write in pink across the top.

Fiona's cousin Barbara-Rose was turning 16 today. And Rose, as people usually called her, had invited Fiona to the party that afternoon. "Aaaaaand," Fiona had said to Frieda all squeakily, "she said you could come, too!"

At that, even Frieda had squeaked like a chew toy. She didn't know Rose that well, but Fiona was always telling the greatest stories about her.

So this morning, while Fiona worked, she told new stories about Rose. And as Frieda listened, she worked on her smoke recipe. Frieda had her ingredients spread out before her. They were the fizziest, spiciest, or loudest foods she could find: pepper, baking soda, vinegar, carbonated water, barbecue potato chips, yogurt (to hold it all together), and one very special ingredient.

In her pocket, Frieda had a wad of spice packets from her favorite meal: Hootin' Hilda's Turtle-Noodle Stew. Hootin' Hilda was, apparently, a cowgirl witch. Her picture was on the package. There she stood, with green skin and pointy hat, wearing cowboy boots and swinging a lasso. On the package it said, "Ya-hoo! You'll go batty for my stew!"

And Frieda *had* gone batty for it. The stew itself had green turtle-shaped noodles, chunks of delicious meat (*not* turtle), and, of course, the fiery spices. Each meal came with two spice packets, and one dash of fiery spice was plenty for Frieda. So she got to keep the extra packets for special occasions—such as today.

Frieda started by shaking some baking soda into a bowl. She added some yogurt. While Fiona talked, Frieda quietly stirred.

"One time at Thanksgiving, I spilled marshmallow yams down Rose's sweater, and she wasn't even mad," Fiona said, sifting her dry ingredients into a bowl. "And she lets me play her guitar, even though I don't know the real way to do it."

Fiona cracked an egg. "You know, Frieda," she said, "I don't think Rose even realizes how wonderful she is. She acts like her beauty and talents are just some magical gift. Did you know that she can make up songs in her head? I guess she writes songs with her new boyfriend. Oooooh." Fiona clapped a little. "I bet we'll get to meet him today."

As Fiona went on, Frieda continued to pour and sprinkle and stir. "Hmmmm," she sighed, staring at her batter. Nothing was even fizzing, never mind smoking. She decided it was time to break open one of the spice packets. She looked in her pocket. Good. She could use one and still have 11 left.

Frieda loved this next part. She found the slit along the packet's edge. Then, with two hands, she riiiiiiipppppped.

*Gurrrgle-glop-glooooop.*

*Splatty-splat-SPLAT.*

Frieda couldn't see what happened next because a wet glob was in her eyes. She felt other wet globs smacking against her bare arms.

"Frieda!" Fiona was shrieking now. "What are you doing?!"

Frieda wiped her eyes. There was her batter. It wasn't rippling or even jiggling. But Fiona's bowl—

"Your Hootin' Hilda's exploded my cake batter!" Fiona cried.

Frieda blinked. Fiona was right. "Oh . . . ," Frieda said. Some of her fiery spices must have gotten flung into the cake batter.

"Ohhhhhh." The seriousness of the situation started to hit Frieda. "Sorry," she said. "Sorry, sorry, sorry, sorry." Her eyeballs started feeling hot and stingy. She had ruined her best friend's special, special cake. "Sorry, sorry, sorry, sorry . . ."

As Frieda went on, Fiona went from furious to angry to annoyed.

"Sorry, sorry, sorry . . ."

"Hmmmph." Fiona let out a big breath. How could she stay angry with Frieda when Frieda was so, so, so sorry? And, after all, it *had* been an accident.

"It's okay," Fiona finally said. She hugged Frieda. "It's okay."

Frieda sniffed. "What now?" she said. "There's no time to start over."

"I know what to do," Fiona said. "Wash up and come with me. We'll clean the kitchen when we come back."

Later the girls would giggle about the disaster. Why did Fiona's cake batter explode while Frieda's smoke recipe just sat there? Who knew? Like many great inventors, the girls had made their discovery by accident. They had stumbled upon an explosive combination—one that would go down in fairy-tale history.

# Chapter 2

**And as** far as disasters went, even Fiona had to admit that this one wasn't *that* terrible. She'd really wanted to make the cake herself but she knew that, as always, Rose would completely understand. They'd buy a cake at Sweet Nothings Bakery instead.

Bells jangled when the girls pushed open the bakery's door. The smell of sugary treats and freshly baked goodies greeted their noses.

"Hello and welcome to Sweet Nothings Bakery, where sticky situations always have a happy ending. My name is Phil. Can I offer you a sample?"

Frieda looked down at her feet and giggled a little. She wasn't used to people in stores talking to her like she was a grown-up. She tried to nudge Fiona, but Fiona was already at the counter. She held her hand over the sample tray like a question mark.

"Why, thank you, Phil," Fiona said. "If only I could decide. They all look so lovely!"

Fiona had gone into princess mode, and it was no wonder. Maybe it was the perfectly clean white apron. Maybe it was the fact that his head was between two giant wedding cakes. Whatever it was, this guy Phil did look, well, princely. And he spoke princely, too.

"Would you care for a sample of our ginger-lemon scone?" Phil held out the tray to Frieda.

"Um, no thanks," Frieda mumbled. She noticed his kind brown eyes. Then she noticed him noticing her noticing. She quickly looked down at his shoes. Her Uncle Chad wore shoes like that. What were they called? Loafers? And were those real polished pennies in them?

The girls walked along the display case. There were short glossy cakes and tall cakes with whipped topping. There was a prickly coconut cake and another in a toasted meringue shell. Each time they pointed, Phil cheerfully described a cake for them: chocolate-raspberry, almond-fudge, and something called lemon chiffon.

"I have decorated these cakes to be simple," Phil explained. "Of course, I can customize them to your taste or write a message across the top."

At that, Fiona pointed to a white chocolate layer cake with apricot filling. "I'll take that one, please. Could you decorate it with 16 roses? And across the top write, 'To my magical cousin.'"

"Certainly," Phil said. He picked up the pastry bag. His eyes went squinty as he carefully squeezed frosting onto the cake.

Frieda gave Fiona a questioning look. "You changed your mind about the words," Frieda said.

"I did," Fiona said, waving her hands above her head. "I guess I was inspired!"

When he was done, Phil boxed up the cake. The white box was so big, it came right up to Fiona's eyes. But she carried it so gracefully that it looked like a prop in her own secret dance routine. Fiona danced with that box straight to the bus stop across the street. With a determined look, she came to a halt under the bus stop sign.

Today was the first time Fiona had ever been in charge of finding her way to Rose's, and she took the responsibility seriously. She'd memorized the way as if it were some secret code her life depended on: Bus 3 past Highway 6, third stop after Vineyard Avenue. Fiona knew just when to pull the string that dinged to tell the driver to stop—right at that mattress store, Dream Right Sleep Emporium.

Today, with her hands so full, Fiona put Frieda in charge of string-pulling duty. The bell dinged, and the bus came to a hissing stop. Soon, the girls were standing on the sidewalk, with their heads tilted back as far as they could go.

Rose lived in a towering skyscraper. Its mirrored face showed the colorful blurs of passing cars, trees, and grass. As the girls walked up to the huge glass doors, their party shoes clicked-clicked on the polished walkway.

On either side of the doors, gardens exploded with color.

"Mmmmm. Smell," Fiona said. Even with her nose behind the cake, she was able to pick up the strong fragrance. She bent over and put her nose in a stalk of frilly yellow flowers.

"*Antirrhinum majus*," Frieda informed her. "Also known as snapdragons."

"Yeah, that's right," Fiona said. She remembered now that Frieda had mistakenly included the flower in a school report she'd done on carnivorous plants. Frieda had felt bad about the mistake, but it was completely understandable to Fiona. After all, the flower looked like a dragon's face. And you could even make it "snap" its mouth by squeezing the flower's sides. It *should* have been a meat-eater, even if it wasn't.

Frieda pulled on one of the doors. "It's locked," she said.

"You have to call first," Fiona said. She pointed her chin at the intercom. "Punch in 4-8-3-2. That's her apartment number—48th floor, top one."

The intercom buzzed and buzzed, but nobody picked up.

Balancing the cake on one hand, Fiona checked her watch. "Five minutes early," she said.

"She's probably so busy getting ready she couldn't answer in time," Frieda said. "I'll try again."

Frieda punched again, and again the intercom buzzed and buzzed.

"Nothing," Fiona said. She looked a little worried.

"The music's probably too loud," Frieda offered. She punched again. Again, the speaker buzzed.

"Hmmm," Fiona said. She sat on the curb by the snapdragons and put the cake in her lap.

What would they do? The ruined cake had been bad enough. Not going to the party was unthinkable. Frieda gnawed at a hangnail. Fiona wound her hair around her fingertip.

*Whooosh.* A gust of air blasted their faces, and the girls looked up. Both glass doors were swung wide open and someone—something?—shot past them. The girls barely got a glance at the figure, wrapped in a shimmering black something-or-other, but the sight made them huddle together.

*Whoosh.* The doors were swinging back together. With the cake in one hand, Fiona jumped up. She caught the doors with her foot.

"Nice work, Fiona!" Frieda said. Now inside, the girls peered through the doors at the figure in black moving away. It seemed to ripple—or was that more like flapping?—in the hazy distance.

"Do you hear that?" Fiona said. A high-pitched, almost-cackling sound wafted in from outside.

"Probably just a siren," Frieda said. She didn't want anything else to ruin her friend's special day. But it was getting harder and harder for Frieda to find explanations, and both girls knew it. Fiona's worry was as obvious as the cake in her hands. Neither girl wanted to be the first to say it, but they both sensed that they were facing a fairy-tale emergency.

# Chapter 3

**At Rose's** door, the girls stared at the gold numerals 4832. Frieda's hands felt as heavy as dictionaries, but she forced herself to lift them to the knocker.

*Tap. Tap. Tap.* The girls waited, but no answer came. Frieda tapped again, and this time the door creaked open by itself. The girls looked at each other. Each girl knew the other's heart was pounding just as fast as her own. Slowly, they pushed open the door and walked in.

"Watch out, Mabel!" Fiona exclaimed.

As Fiona toppled over Rose's dog, the cake box flew onto the carpet. Mabel didn't yelp. She didn't roll over. Fast asleep, the dog just kept on making its gravelly doggy breaths.

The girls poked their heads in the kitchen. There was Fiona's baby cousin George asleep in his high chair. Fiona pointed at the pacifier on the floor. "He should be screaming," Fiona hissed.

Next, they tiptoed into the living room. There, they saw what they both had been dreading. Fiona's Uncle Steve snoozed against the wall with a tray of cheese puffs by his feet. Aunt Linda dozed in a dining room chair with her phone still cradled in her ear. A group of teenage girls flopped over a giant beanbag. Even the digital clock on the mantle had stopped and was flashing 12:00.

Every person—and thing—in Rose's living room was fast asleep—and there was nothing the girls could do to wake them up.

The evidence was too much. The girls had to face the truth.

"Sixteenth birthday . . . ," Frieda slowly said.

"The day of the evil fairy's spell . . . ," Fiona said, gripping Frieda's hand. Both girls thought of the mysterious figure by the door.

"Barbara-Rose, Barbara-Rose . . . ," Frieda chanted in disbelief. "Of course! It sounds just like . . ."

"Briar Rose," Fiona said, "which is another name for . . ."

"Sleeping Beauty!" both girls said together.

The girls dashed around and over the sleeping guests to Rose's bedroom. Fiona flung open the door. It was just like in the fairy tale. Rose was sleeping peacefully on her bed wearing a swoopy white dress. One arm dropped off the bed, and her long, golden hair spread out over her pillow in long, wavy lines.

In front of the bed was a wooden wheel propped up on a thing that looked kind of like an easel.

"A spinning wheel!" Fiona gasped.

Of course! A spinning wheel was a key prop from *Sleeping Beauty*. Last year during a field trip to the colonial museum, Fiona and Frieda had seen a real one from history. They learned that a spinning wheel was an old-fashioned machine for making yarn or thread. On its top, for winding thread, it had a sharp pin called a spindle—another key detail from the fairy tale. During "group explore" time, they'd gone back to the spinning wheel to act out one of their favorite fairy-tale scenes.

Frieda played the evil fairy, one of the greatest evil characters of all time. That evil fairy could really hold a grudge. She was still mad because 16 years before, Sleeping Beauty's parents had invited all the other fairies in the kingdom except her to a party. The party was in honor of the princess, who was just a baby at the time. All the other fairies had taken turns bestowing magical gifts on the baby, like "the gift of beauty" and "the gift of song."

The evil fairy had stormed right into the middle of all this and put a spell on the baby. She'd said that when the princess turned 16, she would prick her finger on a spindle and die, *ah-ha-ha-ha.*

Then, with a puff of smoke and another bone-chilling cackle, the evil fairy had vanished, leaving the guests stunned and dismayed. Luckily, though, one of the good fairies hadn't yet bestowed her gift upon the baby princess. The fairy probably had planned on giving the princess something really great like "the gift of doing back flips." Instead, she had to use up her gift to try to fix the situation.

The good fairy's magic wasn't powerful enough to take away the evil fairy's spell completely, but she could at least make it not so bad. So when the princess turned 16, she would still prick her finger on a spindle. Instead of dying, though, she would fall into a deep sleep.

So they wouldn't miss her too much while she slept, everyone else present in the castle would also nod off until the princess woke up.

Of course, Fiona played Sleeping Beauty, who was completely clueless to all of the above. After the party, the princess's parents had panicked. They'd ordered that all the spinning wheels in the kingdom be burned. (Come to think of it, Fiona's Aunt Linda *had* totally freaked out when Rose had signed up for a class called "The Joy of Old-Fashioned Spinning Wheels" at the community center.) Obviously, the king and queen had never read a fairy tale in their whole lives, because they really thought that they could avoid an evil spell.

Frieda had always thought that Sleeping Beauty should have been allowed to see a spinning wheel. Then she wouldn't have been so amazed when she saw one on her sixteenth birthday. Maybe she would have said, "Why do I want to spin yarn on my birthday when I should be blowing out candles?" But the evil fairy put her into a trance. The trance is where the girls began their scene at the colonial museum.

"You're getting sleepy," Frieda, the evil fairy, said to Fiona, now Sleeping Beauty. Frieda twirled her finger in circles in front of Fiona's face. Fiona moved her head in circles along with Frieda's finger. "Follow me, my little dearie," Frieda said, pointing to the spinning wheel behind the rope.

"Yes, master," Fiona said, walking like a robot up to the rope.

"Now, my pretty chicken," Frieda said, "touch the spindle, touch the spindle, touch the spindle."

"Touch the spindle," Fiona repeated, reaching her hand in the air toward the top of the display.

Then came Fiona's favorite moment: "Aaaaaaa," she shrieked, pretend-sucking the blood off her fingertip. She stood up straight and stretched her arm over her head. Then she crumpled to the floor like a dropped puppet, obviously in a deep, deep sleep.

It was weird. At first the girls had been really scared. But now that they'd seen the spindle and started to remember the fairy tale, something had changed. The girls nodded at each other.

It was time to use their rhyming powers and enter the magic realm of fairy tales. No one was going to ruin Barbara-Rose's sixteenth birthday party. Fiona and Frieda had to set things right!

# Chapter 4

**Luckily, the** girls had prepared a numbered list of rhymes to use in such an emergency.

"Number Five," Fiona said.

"Three, two, one . . . pinky toe," Fiona said, just as Frieda said, "stinky crow."

"Yessss!" Fiona said, as the magic sparkles filled the air. Usually, at this point, the girls would make sure that the rhyme had worked and listen for a second. If it had, all the everyday noises would instantly stop, and only their voices and those of fairy-tale characters could be heard. In this case, though, everyone was already asleep.

Fiona saw the worried look on Frieda's face. She knew her friend hated to skip this step. "We'll just have to trust our powers," Fiona said. That seemed to make Frieda look even more worried, so Fiona decided it was best just to start the action. She sat down on the bed. "Okay, what's our plan?"

Frieda got that look of super concentration that just about any puzzle gave her. She sat cross-legged on the floor. She opened and closed and opened and closed the strap on one of her party shoes.

"Well, not all the books are the same," Frieda slowly said. "We have two choices. Sometimes Sleeping Beauty just wakes up after 100 years . . ."

"In which case we'd have to find a way to speed up time," Fiona added.

"Hmmmmm," Frieda said.

"But in option two, true love's kiss breaks the spell," Fiona went on.

"In that case, we have to find the prince and get him to kiss Rose," Frieda said.

"Okay," Fiona puffed a breath that sent her bangs fluttering. "Let's start there . . . Prince, prince, prince . . . Wait a minute!"

Fiona jumped up. "In some of the books, Sleeping Beauty and the prince are already in love before she falls asleep, which means—"

"Didn't you say that Rose has a new boyfriend?" Frieda interrupted.

"Yes," Fiona jumped a little. "The guy she writes songs with."

"So how do we figure out who he is?" Frieda asked. "Everyone's asleep. There's nobody to ask." She looked at Fiona. Frieda knew her friend's answer, but she wanted Fiona to be the one to say it.

"There's only one way," Fiona said. Why did every fairy-tale emergency have to present some new unpleasant task?

"If you were under a spell by an evil fairy, wouldn't you want her to do it if it could help save you?" Frieda reasoned.

"Of course!" Fiona said. Frieda was right. The stakes were too high. As much as they hated to do it, the girls would have to snoop through Rose's things.

"Okay, Frieda, you begin with the closet," Fiona said. "I'll tackle the drawers."

Luckily, Rose wasn't one to hide her feelings. Once they were clear-headed enough to simply observe their surroundings, the prince's secret identity revealed itself as anything but secret. In fact, his picture was everywhere—in a heart-shaped frame on the desk; pinned to a bulletin board; as part of a collage Rose had made called "My Inspirations."

The girls called out to each other.

"Fiona! Check this out!"

"Frieda! You won't believe it!"

Fiona jumped up and down. Frieda yelled, "woooo-hooooo!" They didn't have to say it. Rose's boyfriend—the prince—was Phil from the bakery!

"Let's go!" Fiona shouted. And out they ran around the sleeping guests, over Mabel, into the elevator, and back to the bus stop by the snapdragons.

When the bus pulled up without a hiss or screech, Fiona turned to her friend. "Still worried about our powers?" she asked.

Frieda smiled. "Not right now." It was so fun being securely within the magic realm of fairy tales—at least for now.

# Chapter 5

**As soon** as they stepped off the bus, Fiona and Frieda heard banging.

"Phil!" Fiona shouted. She pointed to Phil pounding against the giant front windows of Sweet Nothings Bakery.

"Help! Help!"

"We can hear him!" Frieda said. The girls were right on track. If they could hear him, that meant Phil was the real deal.

The girls raced toward the bakery.

Phil was leaning against the bakery window. "What now?" he was saying.

"It's okay," Fiona shouted. "We'll help you."

"Oh, hi," Phil seemed to recognize the girls from earlier in the day. He looked even more disappointed. "No, no, you don't understand," he shook his head. "An evil fairy locked me in here. She took the key. She locked all the windows. I tried calling my manager and the line just rings and rings. There's no way out . . ."

"We can help!" Frieda said.

"No, no. It's so much worse. She put an evil spell on my girlfriend," Phil continued.

"Yes, yes, we know," Fiona said.

"And I'm the only one who can break it!" Phil was starting to panic now.

"We know. We know," Fiona and Frieda shouted together. "We can help!"

Phil leaned away from the glass. He looked at the girls—two third graders with overgrown bangs and baggy socks. Obviously, he'd been expecting a different sort of rescue team. And yet there was a determination in their eyes he must have recognized.

"Who are you?" he asked.

"I'm Fiona," Fiona said.

"And I'm Frieda," Frieda said. "We're fairy-tale experts."

"Really? You can help me?" Phil asked.

"Well . . . ," Fiona said.

"Ummmm," Frieda said.

Now that Phil was looking at them all full of hope and everything, they realized that they weren't exactly sure how to rescue a prince who'd been locked away by an evil fairy.

"Why, yes," Fiona finally said. She was

talking like a princess. Frieda knew this meant her friend was trying to find her nerve.

"We'll just need a minute to, uh, discuss our plan," Frieda said, pulling Fiona over to her side. Seeing how determined her friend was to be brave, Frieda also was determined not to freak out. Besides, there was no time. Rose's birthday was slipping away.

"Okay, think, think, think," they both chanted this time.

Quickly, they reviewed their options.

"Break the lock?" Fiona said. She turned, looked at the bakery door, and shook her head. It was a heavy bolt. "Pick the lock?" she tried. But then Frieda reminded her of the time she forgot her locker combination and they couldn't even pick that dinky lock, no matter how many bobby pins and plastic cards they tried.

"Break the window?" Frieda suggested. But with what? The girls scanned the ground for heavy objects, but the biggest thing they could find was a plastic rabbit from a neighbor's garden. What if they went home and got a hammer? They looked at the giant pane of glass. Would it work? It seemed iffy that they'd be able to outwit an evil fairy with such an ordinary idea.

"Last resort plan," Fiona decided. What else could they do? What else? What else?

Frieda always got the best ideas just from carefully observing her surroundings. So Fiona decided that, instead of twirling her hair around her finger, she'd try that for a change. She walked over to the bakery window. There was the counter, the cash register, the wedding cakes, all the usual stuff. How did Frieda do this anyway?

"Keep looking, keep looking," she told herself.

Meanwhile, in deep concentration, Frieda fiddled with her shoe straps. She cracked her knuckles. She shoved her hands in her pockets. And from her pockets she pulled out—

"Hey! Frieda, look!" Fiona was jumping up and down pointing at something inside the bakery. "Do you still have your Hootin' Hilda's?"

Frieda came running over with the packets in her hand. "Yes!" she said. "Do you see what I think you see?"

"I sure do!" Fiona clapped a little. "Phil!" she shouted. "Bring that giant bowl of cake batter over next to the door."

"Huh?" Phil said.

"Trust us!" Frieda shouted, as she shoved all 11 of the fiery packets under the bakery's thick glass, bolted-shut door.

As the girls explained their plan to the prince, his expression went from confused to worried.

"It's okay," Fiona and Frieda reassured him—even as they reached for each other's hands.

# Chapter 6

**Everything was** in place. The cake batter was by the door. Phil had all 11 spice packets. All he had to do was sprinkle them into the bowl, run away really fast, and—

*Boom-da-BOOM-BOOM-craaaaassshhhhhh.*

The explosion turned out to be even bigger than the girls could have guessed. From behind a tree at the end of the block, they watched in amazement. The entire bakery door went flying across the street and crashed against a stop sign.

"Phil! Phil?" The girls ran toward the bakery. For one moment of panic, they couldn't find Phil. Was he trapped under the rubble? Was he bleeding somewhere in a corner? Had they—had they killed the prince?

But soon their fears were put to rest by the sound of laughing. "Oh man! What a blast!" Phil stepped out of the hole in the front of the bakery. Except for a few globs of batter on his back, he still looked remarkably white and spiffy.

"I spread the batter all around the door's hinges and the lock," he explained. "Then I stood behind the counter and threw the open packets at the door as hard as I could. Then I booked it into the walk-in refrigerator. You know, because of its steel door and all."

"Of course!" Frieda said.

"Why didn't we think of that?" Fiona wondered.

The girls looked at the prince with a new respect. They must have earned his respect, too. For he asked them to come with him on his rescue mission.

"I might need another one of your plans," Phil explained. "Come on!"

Fiona and Frieda followed the prince to the back of the bakery, where he picked up a sparkly black skateboard with neon-orange wheels. Underneath, the skateboard had a picture of a running stallion on it.

"Pile on!" Phil said, handing them each a helmet. He must have noticed Frieda's puzzled look because he explained, "I always keep around a few spare helmets in case of guests."

"Wow, how . . . like a prince," Frieda said, and Fiona giggled.

"All set?" Phil asked, once everyone was on.

"Wait!" Just then Frieda remembered an important detail from the fairy tale. "Hang on!" she shouted, as she ran into the bakery.

She soon returned carrying two cookie sheets and two rolling pins. Frieda could tell from Fiona's and Phil's confused faces that they were trying hard not to say "huh?"

"It was the best I could do," she explained, but they still just looked at her. "See?" she said. She slashed the rolling pin back and forth. "Take that, and that, and that!"

"Ohhhh," Fiona said slowly. "I get it, a sword!" She pointed at one of the cookie sheets. "And a shield!" she said.

"One set for him and an extra set for us," Frieda explained.

"Good idea," Phil said. "You never know what trouble we'll find at the castle." He gripped the rolling pin in one hand and the cookie sheet in the other. The girls grabbed their armor, too. With that, they hopped onto the skateboard,

pushed off, and went to Rose's to break the magic spell.

In the fairy tale in library books, there would be thorny bushes growing all around the castle entrance. All the way to Rose's building Fiona and Frieda wondered—would they get thorny bushes, too? What did the evil fairy have in store for them?

# Chapter 7

**They should** have guessed it.

As the three of them sped past the Dream Right Sleep Emporium, they sniffed the most terrific smell. And up ahead, the skyscraper looked as if it was surrounded by a blaze of yellow.

"The snapdragons!" Frieda cried.

"They're huge!" Fiona said. As they got closer, they saw that the flowers stretched to the building's second row of windows. There must have been hundreds of them, all reflected in the mirrored windows. That cast a bright, cheerful glow around the whole entrance.

The effect was extra creepy. It was like those scary movies where the villain wears a smiley mask. For, in spite of their color and smell, there was nothing at all cheerful about these flowers. Waving on their stalks, the flowers seemed to leer at Phil and the girls. Even worse, the lip-like petals snapped and opened, snapped and opened. The evil fairy had made these giant attack flowers to stop Phil from reaching Rose.

For a minute, Phil, Fiona, and Frieda stood mesmerized by the yellow spectacle. What now?

Phil grabbed his rolling pin tightly by the handle. Then he held up his cookie sheet, but it slipped out of his hand. He tried again. This time he managed to grab it by the edge, but then he seemed stuck. He tried to hold it out and move it around but it kept dropping.

The girls realized that this was one of the few fairy-tale scenes they had never acted out, and so they hadn't worked out all the details. "Of course! You can't use a shield without a handle," Frieda said.

Another problem! Fiona and Frieda ran through their options. He could easily hold the cookie sheet with two hands. But then, what about the sword? Or maybe he could leave the shield? Risky. And besides, every version of *Sleeping Beauty* always showed the prince with both the sword *and* the shield.

Meanwhile, Phil was back on his skateboard. He was riding back and forth holding a cookie sheet over his head with both hands.

"Look!" he said, "If you squat a little, you can keep your balance!"

Luckily, Phil had already proven his smarts. Because if he hadn't, Frieda would be snorting and Fiona would be doing the "crazy" sign. Instead, they watched him with curiosity. Soon, a plan began to take shape in their imaginations.

"That's it! You and Phil go in on the skateboard as fast as you can!" Frieda began.

Fiona continued, "I'll stand behind Phil, holding cookie sheets over both our heads."

"That way I'll have both hands free for the rolling pins," Phil said. "I can bat away the flowers from either side."

"And I'll give you the biggest, fastest push you ever saw," Frieda said.

"You mean—" Phil realized what Frieda was saying. "You're not coming?"

"Not with us," Fiona said. She started getting all teary eyed like a grandma at a piano recital.

"It's your day, Fiona," Frieda said. "And I'll get through as soon as Phil gets in and breaks the spell."

"You sure?" Fiona said. She hugged Frieda.

"Positive," Frieda replied.

And it was an amazing push, if Frieda did say so herself. Phil and Fiona zoomed into the creepy yellowness. He swung wildly with the rolling pins while Fiona held fast to the cookie sheets. Frieda watched the flowers lunge, then coil back. They snapped at the cookie sheets. The plan was working!

"Ha! Ha-ha!" Frieda hooted. They were going to make it! Oh, it felt so good to win. So, so, good—

*AAAAAACCCCK!*

What was that? Who was hurt?

Frieda rushed to the flowers' edge.

*EEEEEEEEEEW.*

That sounded like Phil's voice.

*Grooooossssss.* That was Fiona. Then—*ah-ha-ha-hooooooo.* Hysterical laughter. Definitely both of them.

"Fiona? Phil?" Frieda shouted. "What happened? Are you okay?"

Fiona was laughing so hard she could barely breathe enough to answer.

"We fell off . . . *ha-ha-hic* . . . we're okay . . . *oooooh-ho-heeee* . . . the flowers . . . *snort* . . . they're harmless!"

What? At that, Frieda rushed in.

The flowers had gotten her friends, all right. In fact, the petals were still lapping at Phil and Fiona like giant yellow tongues. And Phil and Fiona slumped in a heap, covered in an oozy, sticky, yellow mess.

As Frieda walked up to her friends, the flowers slimed her, too.

Fiona brushed her sleeve. "It's just pollen and nectar," she explained. "Now you know how bugs feel."

At last it was Frieda's turn to laugh—and finish her victory cheer. It seemed the evil fairy had made the exact same mistake that she had made in her school report. Snapdragons may have looked like meat-eating flowers, but they were not.

"Better luck next time, evil fairy," Frieda shouted. She threw in a cackle, too. It *did* feel so good to win.

# Chapter 8

**Luckily, Phil** knew what code to punch in to make the door open so they didn't have to call upstairs. Soon, the three of them were entering apartment 4832. This time they stepped carefully around Mabel. Fiona led Phil to Rose's room and opened the door. There was the spindle, and there was her cousin, still looking fairy-tale perfect.

As Phil walked in, the girls stood in the hallway. (They'd handled enough fairy-tale adventures by now to know when princes and princesses needed privacy.)

"Ooooh," Fiona let out a little squeak. She bounced on her toes. One of her very favorite fairy-tales scenes—the magic kiss that wakes Sleeping Beauty—was taking place just a few feet away, and with her sweet, special cousin.

Fiona couldn't resist. She just had to peek. Frieda peeked with her.

"What's he doing?" Frieda whispered.

"I, well, I don't know . . . ," Fiona whispered back.

There was Phil, and he was acting as if he'd taken crazy potion. He waved his hands over Rose's face, chanting some mumbly rhyme. Then he clapped three times over her face and said, "Ta-da!"

When that didn't work, Phil blasted the clock radio and put it next to Rose's ear. The alarm of the clock radio blared through the apartment.

*Beep . . . Beep . . . Beep . . .*

"Wake up! Wake up!" he started screaming. Finally, with a huff, Phil turned off the radio.

"Fiona? Frieda?" he called out meekly.

The girls waited a few seconds to answer so it didn't seem as if they'd been right there spying the whole time. "Yes?" they said.

Phil sighed. He ran his hands through his hair. "I know I'm the one who has to break the spell," he said, "but none of my usual spell-breakers are working."

"You mean, you don't know what you're supposed to do?" Frieda giggled.

But Fiona couldn't stand the suspense any longer. "Kiss her, Phil! Kiss her!" she shouted. "Just pucker up and give her a great big smooch!"

At this, Frieda burst out laughing.

"Really?" Phil said. He nodded thoughtfully. "I've never heard of that method, but it sounds interesting. Sure. Kiss her. Why not?"

And with that, Phil leaned over and planted one right on Rose's perfect, candy-pink lips.

Luckily, Phil backed away afterward because a second later, one of Rose's fists was right where his face had been. As she stretched her arms, she let out a giant yawn. She rubbed her eyes and sat up.

"Oh, hi!" She smiled at Fiona, Frieda, and Phil. "Excuse me, I must have dozed off."

Then, she added, "Oh, where are my manners? Phil, this is my cousin Fiona and her best friend Frieda. Fiona and Frieda, this is—"

"We know," Fiona and Frieda said together. Fiona held out her hand and pulled her cousin to

her feet. "In fact, we know *everything,* Rose, and you're safe. The evil fairy can't hurt you now."

Rose gasped. "But how did you—? Really?"

"Trust me," said Fiona. "It's a snappy little story!" At that, Frieda and Phil started laughing.

"Well, I can't wait to hear it!" declared Rose.

She hugged Fiona. "Oh, this is going to be the best birthday ever!"

By then, everyone was waking up in the living room.

"Time for the party!" Fiona declared.

Figuring that many of the guests were not fairy-tale characters, Fiona and Frieda quickly used their rhyming powers to exit the magic realm of fairy tales. After all, they didn't want to miss out on any conversations. Even then, the girls knew they would be talking about—and acting out—this party for months.

Fiona and Frieda didn't want the guests to get freaked out by the spinning wheel. So they pretended that it was their birthday present to Rose. And, as it turned out, Rose was happy to have it. She got to take that "Joy of Old-Fashioned Spinning Wheels" class after all.

Phil and Rose got out some instruments for a jam session. While they made up songs on the guitar, Fiona played back-up on the harmonica. Neither of them seemed to mind that she didn't really know how to play (though some of the other guests might have).

As for the cake, well, a lot of its frosting rosebuds got smooshed when Fiona tripped over Mabel and the box skidded on the carpet. Luckily, Phil knew what to do. With a little

warm water and a butter knife, the cake was as good as new.

That day, Rose made two important decisions. She decided that white chocolate layer cake with apricot filling was her favorite kind. She also secretly decided that she wanted to marry Phil.

Eventually, Fiona and Frieda did tell Rose and her parents the entire story of what happened on Rose's birthday. And, many years later, when Phil and Rose did get married, she chose white chocolate with apricot filling as her wedding cake. Fiona and Frieda baked the cake—this time with no explosions. They decorated it, too. Inside a ring of perfect frosting rosebuds, they wrote, "To a magical couple." And *that* is the story of how the prince and Sleeping Beauty lived happily ever after.

The End

#5. Pinky toe . . .

stinky crow . . .

#17. Porcupine,
ball of twine!

#49. Yum, yum,
bubblegum!